THIS BOOK BELONGS TO:

Leooooo THE LION

This book is dedicated to my family and friends, who love and support me.

To all of the children who have entered my classroom and my heart.

Leo the Lion was a Lion, but like
no Lion ever before,

For this little Lion so small, yet mighty,
hadn't found his roar.

Leo the Lion felt troubled and wanted
to put his mind at ease,

So his search began in the jungle,
amongst the bushes and the trees.

"Hello," said Leo the Lion,
to the Toucan in the tree,

"I'm wondering if you would be
so kind to come and help me?"

"Squawk, squawk," said the Toucan,
high up in the tree.

"My, you don't sound like a lion,
that does surprise me!"

"That's the thing you see," replied Leo,
"I cannot find my roar!",

"I've looked everywhere, high and low,
and even on the floor."

"But my roar is nowhere to be found,
I've looked up, down, left and right,"

"How can I be the king of the jungle,
when I can't give anyone a fright?"

So, the toucan came down from the tree and began to help little Leo look,

But so far, their search wasn't going very well,
they weren't having much luck.

"Hello," said Leo the Lion, to the snake within the grass,

"Could you help my friend and I, with a seemingly impossible task?"

"Hiss, hiss," said the snake,
as he slithered out to see,

"My, you don't sound like a lion,
that does surprise me!"

"That's the thing you see," replied Leo,
"I cannot find my roar!",

"I've looked everywhere, high and low,
and even on the floor."

"But my roar is nowhere to be found,
I've looked up, down, left and right,"

"How can I be the king of the jungle,
when I can't give anyone a fright?"

So, the snake agreed to help his new-found friends, and they continued on their way,

But with no success on their search so far, it was beginning to feel like a long day.

"Hello," said Leo the Lion, to the monkey swinging high,

"I don't suppose you have some free time, to help my new friends and I?"

"Ooh ooh, ah ah," called out the monkey with glee,

"My, you don't sound like a lion, that does surprise me!"

"That's the thing you see," replied Leo,
"I cannot find my roar!",

"I've looked everywhere, high and low,
and even on the floor."

"But my roar is nowhere to be found, I've looked up, down, left and right,"

"How can I be the king of the jungle, when I can't give anyone a fright?"

So, the monkey climbed down from his tree and offered to help his new friend,

Leo was hopeful, now with four sets of eyes,
surely his search was to come to an end.

"Hello," said Leo the Lion, to a sloth snoozing nearby,

"If you're not too busy, we'd love you to help, please say you'll at least try?"

"Yawwwnnn," said the sloth, as he
stretched and clambered out of a tree,

"My, you don't sound like a lion, that does surprise me!"

"That's the thing you see," replied Leo,
"I cannot find my roar!",

"I've looked everywhere, high and low,
and even on the floor."

"But my roar is nowhere to be found,
I've looked up, down, left and right,"

"How can I be the king of the jungle,
when I can't give anyone a fright?"

So, the sloth woke himself
up and joined the search
for Leo's roar,

But what exactly does a roar look like he thought,
as he investigated the jungle floor.

"Hello," said Leo the Lion, to a red-eyed frog who startled him,

"Do you think you could help us too, little frog, our search is rather grim?"

"Ribbit," said the frog, as he looked at Leo woefully,

"My, you don't sound like a lion, that does surprise me!"

"That's the thing you see," replied Leo,
"I cannot find my roar!",

"I've looked everywhere, high and low,
and even on the floor."

"But my roar is nowhere to be found,
I've looked up, down, left and right,"

"How can I be the king of the jungle,
when I can't give anyone a fright?"

So, the frog hopped on over to Leo,
and this made Leo smile,

So many friends he had now, this was the
happiest he'd felt in a while!

The light started to fade, clouds blew over
and drops of rain began to drip,

Leo and his friends snuggled in closer as
the temperature began to dip.

"I don't like this!" squawked the toucan,

"No, me neither!" hissed the snake,

"Our search can't continue!" said the frog,

Sloth and monkey began to shake!

Leo began to wander on, but looked back at the
new friends he had made,

He felt bad leading them so deep in the jungle and
now they were afraid,

This was his opportunity to shine, he knew he had to be brave.

"I can see shelter, this way," he said, as he pointed to a cave.

Just then the animal friends heard a noise; a
rumble, a thunder, a boom!

Then out popped two eyes in the darkness, full
of fire, sharpness and gloom!

"Eeekkkkk!" screeched the toucan,

"Runnnnn!" shouted the frog,

"I want to go home!" cried monkey, as sloth and snake hid behind a log.

Panic drew over Leo, like a wave of despair,
then suddenly "ROOOOARRRRRR!"

he bellowed, like no lion had roared before!

The eyes drew back, the animals cheered, "You've found your roar, yippee!"

"Who'd have thought?" said Leo, "The loudest roar...was always inside of me!"

The friends felt safe as they danced in the rain, and Leo felt mighty and strong,

His search was over, he'd found his roar,
he was the King of the jungle all along!

Printed in Great Britain
by Amazon